亲爱的爸爸妈妈们：

在阅读这本书之前，您可以让您的孩子先在左侧的横线上写下自己的名字——这可能成为他（她）完完整整读完的第一本书，也因此成为真正意义上第一本属于他（她）自己的书。

作为美国最知名的儿童启蒙阅读丛书"I Can Read!"中的一册，它专为刚开始阅读起步的孩子量身打造，具有用词简单、句子简短、适当重复，以及注重语言的韵律和节奏等特点。这些特点非常有助于孩子对语言的学习，不论是学习母语，还是学习作为第二语言的英语。

故事的主角是鼎鼎大名的贝贝熊一家，这一风靡美国近半个世纪的形象对孩子具有天然的亲和力，很多跟贝贝熊有关的故事都为孩子所津津乐道。作为双语读物，它不但能引导孩子独立捧起书本，去了解书中有趣的情节，还能做到真正从兴趣出发，让孩子领略到英语学习的乐趣。

就从贝贝熊开始，让您的孩子爱上阅读，帮助他们开启自己的双语阅读之旅吧！

图书在版编目（CIP）数据

去农场做客：英汉对照 / (美) 博丹(Berenstain,J.) , (美) 博丹 (Berenstain,M.) 著；
姚雁青译. —乌鲁木齐：新疆青少年出版社，2013.1
　（贝贝熊系列丛书）

　ISBN 978-7-5515-2736-1

　Ⅰ.①去… Ⅱ.①博… ②博… ③姚… Ⅲ.①英语－汉语－对照读物②儿童故事
－美国－现代 Ⅳ.①H319.4：I

中国版本图书馆CIP数据核字(2012)第273207号

版权登记：图字 29-2012-24

The Berenstain Bears Down on the Farm
copyright©2006 by Berenstain Bears, Inc.
This edition arranged with Sterling Lord Literistic, Inc.
through Andrew Nurnberg Associates International Limited

贝贝熊系列丛书
去农场做客

(美) 斯坦·博丹　简·博丹　绘著　Stan & Jan Berenstain　　姚雁青　译

出 版 人	徐　江		策　　划	许国萍
责任编辑	贺艳华		美术编辑	查　璇　刘小珍
法律顾问	钟　麟　13201203567（新疆国法律师事务所）			

新疆青少年出版社

（地址：乌鲁木齐市北京北路29号　邮编：830012）

Http://www.qingshao.net　　E-mail：QSbeijing@hotmail.com

印　　刷	北京时尚印佳彩色印刷有限公司		经　　销	全国新华书店
开　　本	787mm×1092mm　　1/16		印　　张	2
版　　次	2013年1月第1版		印　　次	2013年1月第1次印刷
印　　数	1-10000册		定　　价	9.00元
标准书号	ISBN 978-7-5515-2736-1			

制售盗版必究　举报查实奖励:0991-7833932　　版权保护办公室举报电话：0991-7833927
销售热线:010-84853493 84851485　　　如有印刷装订质量问题 印刷厂负责掉换

The Berenstain Bears
I Can Read!

贝贝熊系列丛书 双语阅读

DOWN ON THE FARM
去农场做客

(美) 斯坦·博丹 简·博丹 绘著
Stan & Jan Berenstain

姚雁青 译

CHISO SINCE 1956 新疆青少年出版社

"This way, please.
We are on our way
to visit our friend
Farmer Ben today.

"孩子们，跟我来。
今天我们要去拜访一位朋友，
农场主本先生。

"There's Ben's farm
just up ahead.
As you can see,
it is quite a spread.

"前面就是本先生的农场。
你们看，这个农场真不小。

7

"There's Ben himself
feeding his stock—

"那位就是本先生，
他正在喂他的牲口——

and there's Mrs. Ben
feeding her flock.

"And there's Big Red,
the rooster,
making much ado
about his big, loud
cock-a-doodle-doo."

那位是本太太，
她正在给鸡群撒食。

"那只公鸡叫大红袍，
它打起鸣来可真叫响——
'喔——喔——喔！'"

"Your farm is so big," says Ma,
"as big as can be!
It reaches as far as the eye can see."

"你们的农场可真大。"熊妈妈说,
"大得不得了！大得看不到边儿！"

"Yes, it's a big 'un!" says Ben.
'A hundred acres—
that's ten times ten.

"是的，我们的农场是够大！"本先生自豪地说,
"有十乘十——方圆整整一百英亩哪！

"We grow peas and beans,

"我们种了豌豆和大豆，

and corn and wheat,

还种了玉米和小麦，

and all kinds of other
good things to eat.

各种各样的美食真不赖。

"But we have help—
Shep, our sheepdog,
herds our sheep.

"不过我们干活儿有帮手——
斜坡儿，我们的牧羊狗，赶着羊群跑得欢。

"I cover a lot of ground
in my trusty Jeep.

"我开着好伙计吉普车到处转。

"My scarecrow keeps
the crows away,

"田里有我的稻草人，乌鸦见了都逃散。

and, of course, farm
machines are here to stay.

我的农机真不少，乖乖听从我使唤。

"Our barn cat, Burt,
keeps the mice away.

"我家的猫儿叫博尔特，
老鼠见她蹿得快。

"As for milking——I still like to do it the old-fashioned way.

"要说挤奶呀——老式的挤法我最爱。

"Here, Brother Bear. Give it a try."

"小熊哥哥来来来，你来动手挤个奶。"

Oops! Brother gives Papa
a squirt in the eye.

哎呀呀！牛奶射到熊爸爸的眼里来。

"I have a question,"
says Sister Bear.
"What is that tall thing
over there?"

小熊妹妹问："我想知道，
那个高高的东西是什么？"

"It's the silo," says Ben,
"where we store the wheat
that we sell to folks
who make things to eat.

本先生回答：“那个玩意儿叫筒仓，
我们在里面储存小麦，然后卖给商贩。

"Because wheat's what it takes

小麦做出的东西真不少，

to make the flour

有面粉、

that goes into bread,

面包

cookies,

和饼干，

and cakes."

还能烤出大蛋糕。”

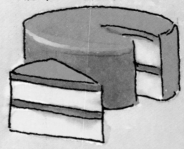

Says Mrs. Ben, "It's lunchtime!
Please take your seats.
Everyone sit down
and have some eats!"

本太太在那头喊："开饭啦!
快请各位来就坐，大家一起吃午餐!"

And what a lunch it is!
Farm-fresh foods of every kind.
For dessert, they munch
watermelon down to the rind.

好丰盛的午餐！
农场食物新鲜又天然。
饭后甜点是西瓜，让大家啃得底朝天。

But Brother has another
question to ask.
"We can see that farming's
a very big task.
My question is this:
Is farming hard
or is it fun?"

可小熊哥哥又提问:"农场的活儿可真不少。
我想知道:干农活累吗? 还是很好玩?"

"Hmm," says Ben.
"Is farming hard
or is it fun?
Well, it's not a job
for everyone.

本先生想了想："干农活是累还是好玩?
嗯，这活儿可不是人人都能干。"

"There are hogs to slop,

"猪儿等着你喂食，

24

horses to feed,

马儿等着你喂草,

fences to mend,

篱笆等着你修补，

gardens to weed,

菜园等着你锄草，

sheep to shear,

羊儿等着剪羊毛，

fertilizer to spread.

牲口的便便要被铲走当肥料。

"But when the sun goes down
and the sky is red—
when the livestock are all
bedded down and fed,
and I sit on the porch with Mrs. Ben—

"可当太阳落山了，天空被染红了，
牛羊都归栏了，牲口都吃饱了，
我和老婆子坐在走廊里——

"Er, What was that question
of yours again?
"Oh yes: Is farming hard or is it fun?

"呃，你的问题是什么来着？
"噢，对了——干农活是累，还是很好玩？

31

"Well, yes, it is hard,
but we love it, son,
So I guess you might say
farming's *hard fun*."

"当然了，干农活很累，
不过，孩子，我们对这事特喜欢，
所以我说啊，
干农活是快乐和辛苦各一半！"